Fuzzy Wuzzy's Big Adventure

Written by Vicki L. Loubier

Illustrated by Charles F. Evers

Fuzzy Wuzzy's Big Adventure

Copyright © 2014 by Vicki L. Loubier

Printed by CreateSpace, an Amazon.com Company

Written by Vicki L. Loubier
Illustrated by Charles F. Evers
~Residents of Maine~

ISBN 13: 978-1495457029

"Hey Mr. Caterpillar, what are you doing in the middle of the road? You are going to be flattened like a pancake if a car comes along and hits you." The blue bird squawked from up on a tree branch.

"Fuzzy Wuzzy, if you please; and if you must know what I am doing, I am trying to get to the other side of the road where my friends are, but it is taking me a very long time because every time a car goes by it rolls me farther away!"

These types of caterpillars, also known as the 'Woolly Bear,' are usually beautifully colored with black ends and reddish-brown colored middles; sometimes though they may be seen of just a solid color.

They also look soft, but actually have stiff bristles of hair. If they are touched they tend to roll up into a ball, as like a protection factor to them.

Many people also believe that the more of the reddish-brown that shows the milder the winter; whereas, the less of the reddish-brown the stormier the winter.

"Almost there. Almost there," Fuzzy Wuzzy kept saying to himself, as he inched closer to the side of the road.

He knew it would be a while but could not give up. Thankfully for him, the last car that went by rolled him real close to the side of the road...

But it took him a while to unroll his body and straighten back out to realize this. When he did though, he was pleasantly surprised.

"So once you finally do get to the other side, what are you going to do, Fuzzy Wuzzy?" The blue bird once again squawked.

"You are quite curious, Mr. Bluebird, but if you must know – once I find my friends, we need to find winter coverage.

I just hope they are where I can see them. I am very tired. This has been a long day."

Before inching along much further, Fuzzy Wuzzy needed some food.

He found a clover patch close by which is just what he needed, as these caterpillars are very fond of this, and it also supplies them with plenty of water.

He was fortunate to find a big clover too, which made him very happy and gave him the energy to continue on.

After taking a while having a satisfying 'feast,' he heard a happy sound...

"Fuzzy, Fuzzy, we are over here. Do you see us?"

It took a few moments for him to focus but then did see them and replied back, "I do see you all and will be there soon."

His friends were not far away.

They were on some leaves and

branches within a foot from him,

but for him would take a while to

get to. They all watched as he

inched along at his quickest pace
towards them.

He finally reached his friends
after what seemed like forever and
joined them on the leaves.

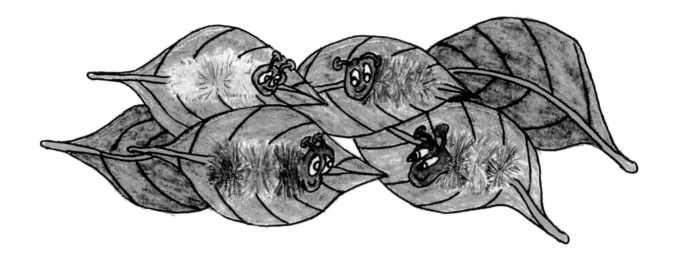

"I am soooo happy to have finally reached all of you so we are all together again, as we need to prepare and decide where we will meet after our transition. Now though, it is time for me to rest for a while. This has been quite the

adventure for me. I hope you all

understand."

No sooner did he say those words, he was dozing off to sleep but with one more sentence before he was finally out, "See you all in the spring."

"We are all glad you finally arrived, Fuzzy Wuzzy, and now we can all be at ease. Rest well, and see you in the spring."

The last sound he heard before dozing off completely was the sound of the blue bird squawking once again in the tree.

He knew that was the blue birds' good-bye too.

Fuzzy Wuzzy got some rest and when he awoke, slowly inched along with the others. None of them were saying a word.

They all knew that they needed to find some bark to cover themselves under; or logs with holes so they could crawl in for the winter.

Because, just like real bears, these Woolly Bears hibernate too!

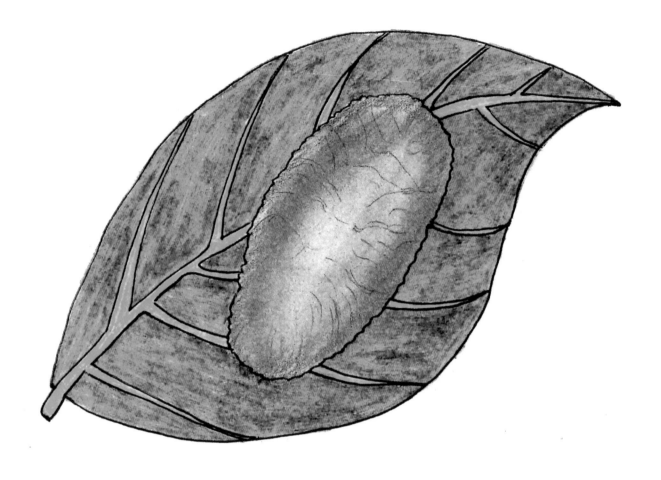

These Woolly Bear Caterpillars spin

a cocoon and transform inside them

into a full-grown moth in the spring

called the Isabella Tiger Moth,

which can be of a yellowish-orange

color with black spots on its cream

colored wings...such as this.

Spring arrived and after many months of winter hibernation, the four of them awoke. The transformation phase was just about done. They were still all together but of totally different shapes.

Still recognizing each other, they said their good-byes as they knew that was how it had to be now; and off they flew onto their own new adventures.

About the Author

Vicki L. Loubier resides in Maine with her husband and two children. She has written two other books, both published in 2013. Her work consists of Young Adult and Children's books. She works full-time, but enjoys writing in her spare time.

Other published books by Vicki L. Loubier

EXPOSED- Young Adult

THE HALLOWEEN PRINCESS – Children's

THE FOLLOWING – Young Adult

–Sequel to EXPOSED-

(to be released in 2014)

Made in the USA
Charleston, SC
01 March 2014